S0-CYE-276

Thank you to the generous team who gave their time and talents to make this book possible:

Author
Elizabeth Spor Taylor

Illustrator
Elizabeth Spor Taylor and the young Ethiopian women affiliated with the Banana Art project in Jimma, Ethiopia

Creative directors
Caroline Kurtz, Jane Kurtz, and Kenny Rasmussen

Translator
Alem Eshetu Beyene

Designer
Beth Crow

Ready Set Go Books, an Open Hearts Big Dreams Project

Special thanks to Ethiopia Reads donors and staff for believing in this project and helping get it started-- and for arranging printing, distribution, and training in Ethiopia.

Copyright © 2020 Ready Set Go Books

ISBN: 978-1676985433
Library of Congress Control Number: 2020922031

All rights reserved.
No part of this book may be reproduced, scanned or distributed in any printed or electronic form without permission. Printed in Seattle, WA, U.S.A.

Republished: 11/08/20

I Hide

ተደብቄያለሁ

English and Amharic

Good morning!
What will I do today?

እንደምን አደራችሁ?
ዛሬ ምን ላድርግ?

I will hide and see the birds as they sing. I will see them, but they will not see me.

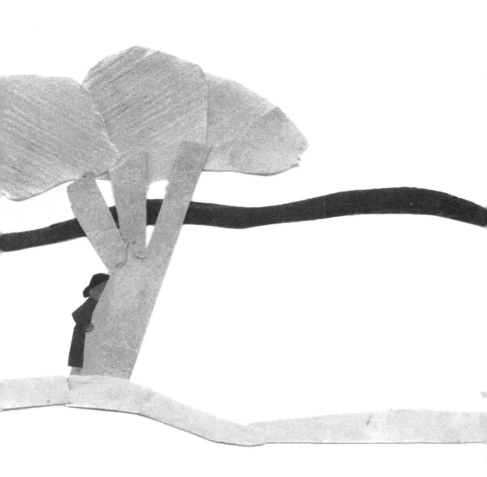

እደበቅና ወፎቹ ሲዘምሩ
እመለከታቸዋለሁ። አያቸዋለሁ፤
እነርሱ ግን አያዩኝም።

I will hide and see people as they walk. I will see them, but they will not see me.

እደበቅና ሰዎቹ ሲሄዱ
እመለከታቸዋለሁ። አያቸዋለሁ፤
እነርሱ ግን አያዩኝም።

I will hide and see people planting trees. I will see them, but they will not see me.

እደበቅና ሰዎቹ ዛፍ ሲተክሉ
እመለከታቸዋለሁ። አያቸዋለሁ፤
እነርሱ ግን አያዩኝም።

I will hide and see my mother cooking. I will see her, but she will not see me.

እደበቅና እማማ ምግብ ስታበስል
እመለከታታለሁ። አያታለሁ፤ እርሷ
ግን አታየኝም።

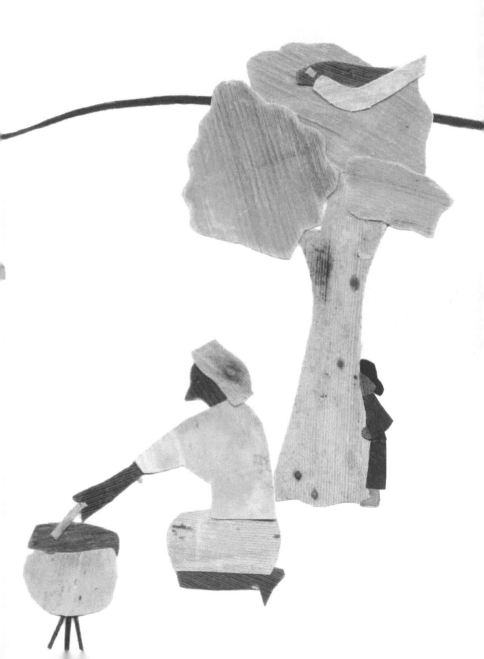

I will hide and see the respected elder with his umbrella. I will see him, but he will not see me.

እደበቅና አባ ጃንጥላቸውን ይዘው
እመለከታቸዋለሁ፡፡ አያቸዋለሁ፤
እርሳቸው ግን አያዩኝም፡፡

I will hide and see the family walking. I will see them, but they will not see me.

እደበቅና የአንድ ቤተሰብ አባላት ሲሄዱ እመለከታቸዋለሁ። አያቸዋለሁ፤ እነርሱ ግን አያዩኝም።

I will hide and see a traveler and a donkey. I will see them, but they will not see me.

እደበቅና መንገደኛውንና አህያዋን
እመለከታቸዋለሁ። አያቸዋለሁ፤
እነርሱ ግን አያዩኝም።

I will hide and see the woman pouring coffee. I will see her, but she will not see me.

እደበቅና ሴትዬዋ ቡና ስትቀዳ
እመለከታታለሁ፡፡ አየታለሁ፤ እርሷ
ግን አታየኝም፡፡

I will hide and
see the man
and his sheep.
Oh no! I can
see him and he
can see me!

እደበቅና ሠውዩውንና በጎቹን
እመለከታቸዋለሁ። ውይ! ጉድ ፈላ!
ሳየው እርሱም አየኝ።

I hope that no one finds me hiding tomorrow. Good night.

ነገ ከምደበቅበት ማንም እንደማያገኘኝ
ተስፋ አደርጋለሁ። ደህና እደሩ።

About The Story

This book was inspired by banana leaf art created in Jimma, Ethiopia by young Ethiopian women. While wandering the stalls in a market in Addis Ababa, the author of this book, came upon greeting cards depicting Ethiopian countryside scenes made from parts of banana trees. She was intrigued by the familiar scenes and interesting medium. With thoughts of using them to send messages to friends, she bought one of each card, but found she could not part with them. They stayed preserved in their plastic sleeves until years later, when she saw them from a different perspective. This time, she spread the cards out and looked at them together and played with their arrangement, until the art began to tell a story.

About the Author

Elizabeth Spor Taylor is an international literacy specialist who served as writer and editor of English learning materials for Ethiopian students. She has traveled to Ethiopia eleven times visiting schools and working collaboratively with Ethiopian educators throughout the country. Elizabeth became familiar with the successes of Ethiopia Reads while touring sponsored libraries in various regions of Ethiopia. Her expertise is in primary grades literacy relative to native English speakers as well as English Speakers of Other Languages. She is a contributing member of the Book Centered Learning Committee for Ethiopia Reads and supports the advancement of English skills within the refugee population in Cleveland, Ohio.

Elizabeth among English for Ethiopia textbooks as they are printed and assembled in Addis Ababa.

About the Illustrators

Jimma Banana Art was an organization started in 2000 with the intent to provide work for approximately 30 young women living in Jimma, Ethiopia. Banana trees are plentiful in Jimma and provided an accessible and sustainable medium for the artists. Different parts of the banana plant were dried, ironed, and baked to create varying colors and textures. These materials were then cut into patterns and glued onto paper in designs that depicted local landscapes and traditional scenes.

In order to complete the story, more art was needed for illustrations. The author searched the internet. In addition to finding other images of greeting cards created by the Jimma Banana Art organization, she found banana art produced by various Ethiopian artists. Using their art as a basis for design, Elizabeth used construction paper and color copies of banana tree materials to piece and glue together collages. These collages, along with the original banana art greeting cards purchased in the market in Ethiopia, completed the story.

About Ready Set Go Books

Reading has the power to change lives, but many children and adults in Ethiopia cannot read. One reason is that Ethiopia doesn't have enough books in local languages to give people a chance to practice reading. Ready Set Go books wants to close that gap and open a world of ideas and possibilities for kids and their communities.

When you buy a Ready Set Go book, you provide critical funding to create and distribute more books.

Learn more at:
http://openheartsbigdreams.org/book-project/

About Ethiopia Reads

 Ethiopia Reads was started by volunteers in places like Grand Forks, North Dakota; Denver, Colorado; San Francisco, California; and Washington D.C. who wanted to give the gift of reading to more kids in Ethiopia. One of the founders, Jane Kurtz, learned to read in Ethiopia where she spent most of her childhood and where the circle of life has come around to bring her Ethiopian-American grandchildren. As a children's book author, Jane is the driving force behind Open Hearts Big Dreams Ready Set Go Books - working to create the books that inspire those just learning to read.

About Open Hearts Big Dreams

 Open Hearts Big Dreams began as a volunteer organization, led by Ellenore Angelidis in Seattle, Washington, to provide sustainable funding and strategic support to Ethiopia Reads, collaborating with Jane Kurtz. OHBD has now grown to be its own nonprofit organization supporting literacy, innovation, and leadership for young people in Ethiopia.

Ellenore Angelidis comes from a family of teachers who believe education is a human right, and opportunity should not depend on your birthplace. And as the adoptive mother of a little girl who was born in Ethiopia and learned to read in the U.S., as well as an aspiring author, she finds the chance to positively impact literacy hugely compelling!

About the Language

Amharic is a Semetic language -- in fact, the world's second-most widely spoken Semetic language, after Arabic. Starting in the 12th century, it became the Ethiopian language that was used in official transactions and schools and became widely spoken all over Ethiopia.

It's written with its own characters, over 260 of them. Eritrea and Ethiopia share this alphabet, and they are the only countries in Africa to develop a writing system centuries ago that is still in use today!

About the Translation

Alem Eshetu Beyene taught translation at Addis Ababa University for three years and translated six books during that time. He also has taught Amharic and written a book titled Amharic For Foreign Beginners. In addition, he has published a number of books for children that can be found in bookshops in Addis Ababa (and two on Amazon.com) and in schools where he donates copies for families that cannot afford to buy them.

Find more Ready Set Go Books on Amazon.com

 Chaos

 Not Ready!

 We Can Stop the Lion

 Talk Talk Turtle

 The Glory of Gondar

 Giraffe and Me

 Fifty Lemons

 Big, Bigger, Biggest

*To view all available titles, search
"Ready Set Go Ethiopia" or scan QR code*

CPSIA information can be obtained
at www.ICGtesting.com
Printed in the USA
LVHW070008040622
720468LV00001B/3